This Little Tiger book belongs to:

_____

_____

_____

To my father-in-law
grumpy grandad Len
- S. S.

For G. R. hero
with love
- C. B.

LITTLE TIGER PRESS

1 The Coda Centre, 189 Munster Road, London SW6 6AW
www.littletigerpress.com

First published in Great Britain 2009
by Little Tiger Press, London
This edition published 2012

Text copyright © Steve Smallman 2009
Illustrations copyright © Cee Biscoe 2009

Steve Smallman and Cee Biscoe have asserted their rights
to be identified as the author and illustrator of this work under
the Copyright, Designs and Patents Act, 1988

Printed in China

10 9 8 7 6 5 4 3 2 1

# GRUFF the GRUMP

Steve Smallman     Illustrated by Cee Biscoe

LITTLE TIGER PRESS

Gruff was a bear.

A great big bear.

A great big, scowly, growly, grizzly grump of a bear.

He lived all alone in a musty, dusty old cave where nobody
ever came to visit.

The other animals hid when they saw him coming.
They called him 'Gruff the Grump'.
"HUMPH!" went Gruff the Grump,
to show he didn't care.

One morning, Gruff the Grump was
stomping through the forest when
he saw something strange . . .

It was a small, upside-down rabbit,
high in the branches of a tree.

"Hello, Mr. Bear," said the rabbit, upside-downly.
"I'm a bit stuck. Can you help me down please,
thank you very much?"

"HUMPH!" scowled Gruff the Grump,
and he turned to walk away.

"Oh please, Mr. Bear, PLEEEEEEASE get me down!"
pleaded the rabbit.

Much to Gruff the Grump's surprise, he
found himself lifting the little rabbit
gently down to the ground.

"Thank you, thank you, Mr. Bear," said the rabbit.
"There was a fallen star caught in the tree so I had
to rescue it, but then I got stuck and then you
had to rescue me.

"Here," she said
with a smile,
"you can have it."

She carefully put the fallen star in the old bear's
huge, hairy paw and hopped off home.

Gruff the Grump thought that the 'star' looked
a lot like a leaf, but he took it home anyway
and put it on his mantelpiece.

It was so golden and beautiful that it made him realize
just how musty and dusty his cave had become.

And for the first time in a very long time, he
dusted the mantelpiece and brushed away
some of the cobwebs.

A few days later, Gruff the Grump was fishing
in the river when a log floated past. Clinging to the log
was a small, soggy rabbit holding an orange pointy thing.
   "Hello, Mr. Bear," said the little rabbit, soggily.
"Can you help me out of the water please, thank
   you very much?"

"Humph!" went Gruff the Grump.
But then he reached over to lift the little
rabbit safely onto the riverbank.

"Thank you, thank you, Mr. Bear,"
said the rabbit. "There was a fallen star
in the water, and I had to rescue it.
You are very big and very kind.
Will you look after it for me?"

But Gruff the Grump just turned
and lumbered away. He was feeling
a bit funny. Nobody had ever, ever
called him 'kind' before.
"But Mr. Bear, Mr. Bear,
come back!" cried the little
rabbit, running after him.
"I can't look after it
on my own!"

"OKAY, OKAY,
I'LL TAKE IT!"
snarled Gruff the Grump.
And snatching the star,
he slammed his
cave door
behind him.

Gruff the Grump put the star on the mantelpiece
next to his other star. They looked so clean and
colorful that they made him realize just how grim
and grimy his cave still was.

So for the first time in a very long time, he swept
up all the old pine needles from the floor.

Now his cave was very clean.
But it was bare and empty inside,
and suddenly Gruff felt like a
bear who was empty inside too.
He started to feel sad . . .

And when he'd finished feeling
sad, he started to feel cross . . .

And he was right in the middle
of feeling cross when there
was a knock on the door.
"WHAT IS IT NOW?"
he shouted.

It was the little rabbit with a whole barrow full of stars.

"Hello, Mr. Bear," she said worn-outly.

"There were lots and lots of fallen stars and I had
to rescue them . . ."

"GO AWAY!" Gruff the Grump roared.
"I DON'T WANT ANY MORE
STUPID STARS!"

Then to his great surprise,
the little rabbit burst into tears.

Gruff the Grump felt terrible.
He wanted the little rabbit
to stop crying, but he didn't
know what to do. He tried
pulling silly faces . . .
But that didn't work.

He did a funny dance . . .
But that didn't work either.

Then he sat down next to her and said:
"I'm sorry I shouted at you, little rabbit.
I really am a grizzly old grump of a bear."

The little rabbit stopped crying and tried
a little smile. And for the first time in a very
long time, Gruff the Bear smiled, too!

Gruff and the little rabbit scattered the stars
around the cave, laughing out loud as they fell
like fiery snowflakes all about them.

The little rabbit stayed and played with Gruff
until nearly bedtime.

"I have to go now," she said sadly.

"Will you come again soon?" asked Gruff.
"Very soon!" the little rabbit smiled.
Then she kissed him goodnight
and hopped off home.

Gruff the Bear gave a great big yawn and snuggled
down to sleep in his warm, starry bed.
And for the first time in a very long time,
**he was happy.**